# Dear Parent:

Congratulations! Your child is taking the first steps on an exciting journey. The destination? Independent reading!

**STEP INTO READING**® will help your child get there. The program offers five steps to reading success. Each step includes fun stories and colorful art. There are also Step into Reading Sticker Books, Step into Reading Math Readers, Step into Reading Write-In Readers, Step into Reading Phonics Readers, and Step into Reading Phonics First Steps! Boxed Sets—a complete literacy program with something for every child.

## Learning to Read, Step by Step!

**Ready to Read** Preschool–Kindergarten
• big type and easy words • rhyme and rhythm • picture clues
For children who know the alphabet and are eager to begin reading.

**Reading with Help** Preschool–Grade 1
• basic vocabulary • short sentences • simple stories
For children who recognize familiar words and sound out new words with help.

**Reading on Your Own** Grades 1–3
• engaging characters • easy-to-follow plots • popular topics
For children who are ready to read on their own.

**Reading Paragraphs** Grades 2–3
• challenging vocabulary • short paragraphs • exciting stories
For newly independent readers who read simple sentences with confidence.

**Ready for Chapters** Grades 2–4
• chapters • longer paragraphs • full-color art
For children who want to take the plunge into chapter books but still like colorful pictures.

**STEP INTO READING**® is designed to give every child a successful reading experience. The grade levels are only guides. Children can progress through the steps at their own speed, developing confidence in their reading, no matter what their grade.

Remember, a lifetime love of reading starts with a single step!

*To Hamlet*
*(my guinea pig when I was*
*the same age as Pinky Dinky Doo),*
*and to Frisky*
*(my daughter's hamster).*
*Thank you for inspiring Mr. Guinea Pig.*

Special thanks to Katonah Elementary School
and to Lewisboro Elementary School

Photography by Sandra Kress

Digital coloring and compositing by Paul Zdanowicz



www.stepintoreading.com

Educators and librarians, for a variety of teaching tools, visit us at
www.randomhouse.com/teachers

*Library of Congress Cataloging-in-Publication Data*
Jinkins, Jim.
Pinky Dinky Doo : back to school is cool! / written and illustrated by Jim Jinkins.
p. cm. — (Step into reading. A step 3 book)
SUMMARY: When her little brother, Tyler, is nervous about his first day of school, Pinky Dinky Doo tells him a story about the time she and her friends had really bad hair days when school pictures were scheduled.
ISBN 0-375-83236-X (trade) — ISBN 0-375-83237-8 (pbk.) — ISBN 0-375-93237-2 (lib. bdg.)
[1. Brothers and sisters—Fiction. 2. Storytelling—Fiction. 3. First day of school—Fiction. 4. Schools—Fiction. 5. Hair—Fiction.]
I. Title. II. Series.
PZ7.J57526Bac 2005 [E]—dc22 2004010476

Printed in the United States of America 10 9 8 7 6 5 4 3 2

by Jim Jinkins

Random House New York

This is my family.
Mommy Doo
Daddy Doo
Mr. Guinea Pig
Tyler Doo
Pinky Dinky Doo
Daffinee Toilette
These are my friends.
Nicholas Biscuit
Bobby Boom

Woo-hoo!

It was the first day
back to school
from summer break.
"Back to school rules!"
Pinky shouted.
"Back to school drools,"
Tyler said.

“Come on, little brother,
time to get dressed,” said Pinky.
“I’m not going,” Tyler said.
He pulled the covers over his head.
“You are too,” said Pinky.
“I am not,” said Tyler.

NOT
ARE TOO!
AM NOT!
ARE TOO!
R2
AM NOT!
ARE TOO
NOT
R2
R2
NOT
AM NOT
ARE TOO!
AM NOT!
ARE TOO
NOT
AM NOT!
ARE TOO!
NOT
AM
R2
AM NO
ARE TOO
NOT
T!
AM NOT!
R2
ARE TOO!
NOT
NOT
AM NOT!
R2
NOT
NOT
R2
NOT
ARE T

“Tyler!
Hurry up,”
Mom shouted up the stairs.
“The big bus will be here soon!”
Tyler yelped and disappeared
somewhere in the laundry.

Pinky noticed that the clothes
were shaking.
"Wow, Tyler,
you're shaking like you're . . .
what's that word
that means you're
really nervous?
What's that
word that means
you're totally
worried?"

“Apprehensive?”

Tyler said from under the laundry.

“That’s it!”

said Pinky.

“That’s the word I’m looking for.”

"So you're apprehensive about the first day in the first grade?" Pinky asked.

All Tyler could do was touch his nose—which anybody knows means Pinky was right on the nose.

"That gives me an idea!"
said Pinky.

"Are you going to make up
one of your stories?"
Tyler asked.

"Yesserooni positooni!"
Pinky said.

Yesserooni positooni!

Yesserooni positooni!

"I'll just shut my eyes,

wiggle my ears,

and crank up my imagination,"

said Pinky.

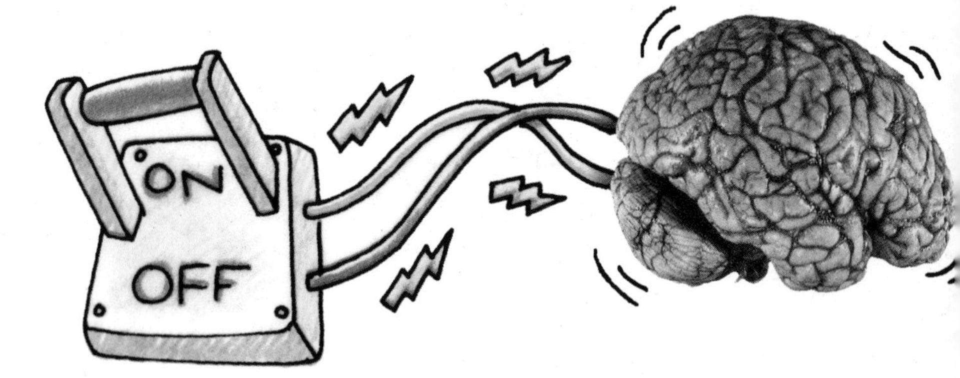

"The name of this story is . . ."

It was a no-big-deal,
regular day at

Great Big School.

NOT!

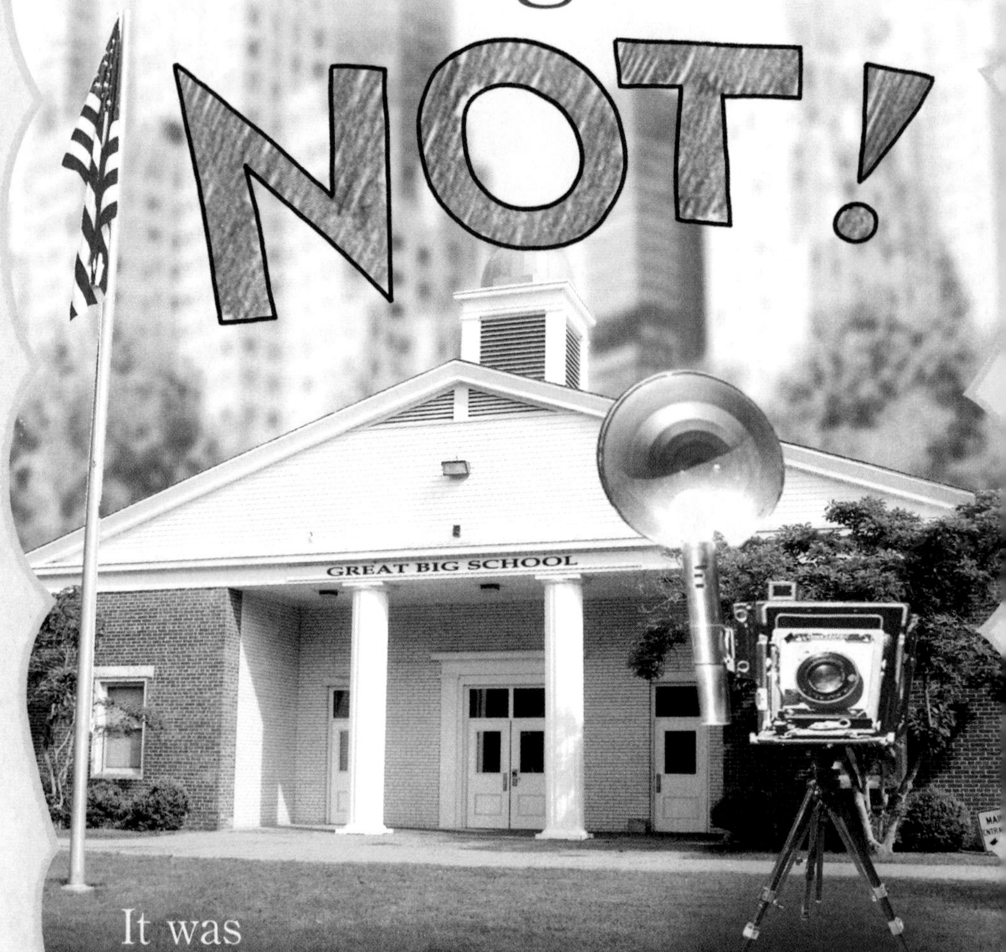

GREAT BIG SCHOOL

It was

School Picture Day!

It was the only day
of the whole school year
when everyone wanted
to look their absolute best.

But that morning,

when Pinky looked in the mirror,

her eyes nearly popped

out of her head!

Her hair looked like:

A A tornado

had hit it.

B

Two cats had

had a fight

on her head.

C It was spooky

haunted.

D All of the above.

The answer is D.
And D stands for Pinky Dinky's
Big Bad Hair Doo!
That is definitely a Pinky Dinky Don't!

Pinky was worried
about having her picture taken
with such a bad hairdo!

But Pinky was not the sort of person to lie down when problems came up. So she and Mr. G got busy.

At first Mr. G
tried to pull
her hair up.

Then he tried
to comb
it down.

It worked for a second,
but then—

BOI-YOI-
YOING!

Finally,
Pinky decided that
she would have to wear a hat
to School Picture Day.

So she spring-loaded
her Big Bad Hair
into a shiny hat.

At school,

Pinky noticed that

Nicholas Biscuit

was also wearing

a big hat.

The fake beard made him look like Abe Lincoln!

Normally,

Nicholas would comb

his hair into a pointy triangle.

But today his hair made

a quadrilateral.

"Quah-druh-LAT-er-ul"
"Quad" means "four" and "lateral" means "with sides."

2
1
3
4
Today

BOOK OF BIG WORDS

Which shape is a quadrilateral?

A Underpants

B The Statue of Liberty

C A banana

D A rectangle

Pinky looked around
for Daffinee Toilette.
"Daffinee will know what to do,"
Pinky said.
"Her hair is always perfect."

They found Daffinee.
Sure enough, her hair was perfect.

That is,
until she turned sideways.

Behind the cutout
was a hairdo disaster.
It looked like Daffinee
was going 80 mph
while standing still!

When Pinky,
Nicholas,
and Daffinee
got to the classroom,
it looked empty.

Everyone was hiding
because they
were all having
a bad hair day.

Even Ms. Maganza and
Principal Dipthong
were having problems.

And it was School Picture Day!
Everybody was reeeeally
apprehensive.

Pinky knew her friends were upset.

So she decided to Think Big!

Usually, Pinky had an everyday,

normal, kid-sized brain.

That is, until she decided to think big!

She thought

and thought

and thought.

This time as she thought,
her head didn't grow
any bigger at all . . .

but her hair sure did.

Pinky Dinky's Hair Doo
grew bigger and
BIGGER and BIGGER
until the classroom
looked like
a shady rain forest.

And then it happened . . .

DI

Pinky had a big idea.

She said,

"Hey, I know

what we can do . . .

**A** We can all shave our heads.

**B** We can knit our hair into sweaters just in time for winter.

**C** We can just GET OVER IT and have our pictures taken anyway!"

The answer was C, of course.

Everybody decided to just get over it and make the best of a bad hairdo situation.

They came out of hiding
and took off their hats
and hair cutouts.

Then they marched
to the gym,
where Mr. Pixel was waiting
to take their school picture.

And just as you might have guessed,
that class picture was
the funniest
class picture
ever taken.

Now, that's
something you don't
see every day!

Nobody ever expected
to end up laughing on
a Bad Hair Day.
But they did.
And nobody
was apprehensive
ever again.

POOF!

"And that's *exactly* what happened . . . pretty much."

BEEP! BEEP! BEEP!

"Hey, that's the school bus,"
said Pinky.
"Oh no," Tyler said.
"I don't want to go on the bus!"

“Come on, Tyler,” Pinky said.

“You can sit next to me.

We ride the big school bus

together, remember?”

“Oh yeah,” Tyler said happily.

"Hurry up . . . ,"
said Pinky.

I'll miss you.

"Last one on the bus has

Big Bad Hair!"

I bet you can make up a story, too!
EMERGENCY EXIT
THE END
ICU2 - OU812
STATE LAW PROHIBITS SCHOOL BUS FROM TURNING RIGHT ON RED